EXPLORER ACADEMY

NATIONAL
GEOGRAPHIC

EXPLORER ACADEMY

ULTIMATE
ACTIVITY CHALLENGE

| SOLVE PUZZLES | TRAVEL THE WORLD |
UNCOVER MYSTERIES TO COMPLETE YOUR MISSION!

TRACEY WEST AND DR. GARETH MOORE

NATIONAL GEOGRAPHIC
WASHINGTON, D.C.

SO **YOU** WANT
TO BE AN *EXPLORER*

Find out if you've got what it takes to make it at Explorer Academy! In this book you'll find more than 80 awesome activities that challenge your skills in codebreaking, problem solving, puzzle cracking, and general expertise in flexing your mental muscle out in the field.

Don't worry if you can't figure something out. Explorers Cruz, Emmett, Sailor, and Bryndis will pop up along the way to offer tips and share some fun facts about your adventures! But beware: You might also encounter agents from the mysterious Nebula, an evil organization out to get Cruz and his friends—and maybe you, too!

Let's get going, recruit— there's no time to waste! The only thing stopping you from completing these missions (other than Nebula) is an unsharpened pencil.

LOOK FOR TIPS AND FUN FACTS ALONG THE WAY FROM THESE EXPLORER ACADEMY RECRUITS:

// CRUZ //

// EMMETT //

// SAILOR //

// BRYNDIS //

DURING YOUR TRAINING, YOU'LL ENCOUNTER THESE PUZZLES ...

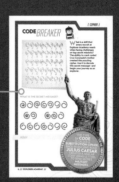

Spot the Difference You'll need keen powers of observation to circle the differences you find between two pictures that otherwise look identical.

Codes and Ciphers Use code keys or other clues to decipher secret messages. A cipher is a way of transforming information to hide its true meaning.

Sudoku and Letter Sudoku Wield your reasoning skills and the process of elimination to fill in grids with numbers and letters.

Number Pyramids Using logic and your super skills of addition and subtraction, fill in the blank squares so that the value of each square is equal to the sum of the two numbers directly below it.

Word Fit Puzzles This is kind of like a crossword puzzle—but without clues. Instead, you have to figure out how all the words you're given fit inside the empty squares.

... and so much more! You'll be challenged by crosswords and word searches, logic problems and word scrambles, and letter swaps and connect the dots. You'll make your way through maps and mazes to solve mysteries. And get ready to show your creative side with art and drawing activities.

ARE YOU **STUCK** AND **NEED A HINT?** FIND ALL THE **SOLUTIONS** AT THE BACK OF THE BOOK!

CODE *BREAKER*

hat is a skill that every recruit at Explorer Academy needs when facing challenges on top secret missions? The ability to crack codes! Cruz Coronado's mother created this puzzling cipher. Use it to decode this secret message—and begin your journey as an explorer.

A B C D E F G H
I J K L M N O P
Q R S T U V W X
Y Z 0 1 2 3 4 5
6 7 8 9 . , ! ?

WHAT IS THE SECRET MESSAGE?

ANSWER

THIS TYPE OF **CODE** IS CALLED A **SUBSTITUTION CIPHER.** BACK IN ANCIENT ROME, **JULIUS CAESAR** CREATED A SIMILAR CODE USING LETTERS TO SEND SECRET **MILITARY MESSAGES.**

STOKED TO SURF

Cruz and Bryndis both love to surf. Check out the surfing terms and slang in the glossary. Then see if you can find them hidden in the puzzle. Circle all the terms you find.

```
S A A O B A C K H A N D I L F
D R N O L L I E G N I L G N A
G E R A O T H A N G T E N A A
O T K E F O R E H A N D S L H
O F R O G H E N I H A W O A S
F E H S T G K A T Y A H R M L
Y K G B H S O T R U A L R H L
F D T R N O A H L N O A B O A
O T I A B K R A H S R E N A X
O O S O E T I T G E O G P B E
T S I O H R L N B L B N B I D
A A F O E A A B R O A O O K W
S F I A Y R U A A L A S E O O
R A I L L R N R O R A R S O A
N A G Y L O D T E D A O D Y E
```

AERIAL
ALOHA
ANGLING
AXED
BACKHAND
FOREHAND
GLASSY
GNARLY
GOOFY FOOT
HANG TEN
HOGGER
LONGBOARD
NOLLIE
RAIL
RUBBER ARMS
SHARK BAIT
SHORTBOARD
STOKED
TAIL
TAKEOFF
WAHINE
WIPEOUT

GLOSSARY

AERIAL A surfing move. A wave sends the surfer and board into the air, and the surfer lands on the same wave.

ALOHA Hawaiian for hello and goodbye

ANGLING When a surfer rides across the wave at an angle toward the shoreline

AXED When a surfer wipes out after being hit by the lip of the wave

BACKHAND To surf with your back to the wave

FOREHAND To surf with your face to the wave

GLASSY Smooth seas

GNARLY Big, intense waves

GOOFY FOOT To surf with your right foot forward on the board

HANG TEN To surf with your ten toes over the nose of the board

HOGGER A surfer who rides all the waves

LONGBOARD A wide, thick surfboard usually longer than 8'6"

NOLLIE Awesome!

RAIL The edge of the surfboard

RUBBER ARMS When your arms feel weak after paddling

SHARK BAIT The surfer farthest away from the shore

SHORTBOARD A short, narrow surfboard

STOKED Excited

TAIL The rear end of the surfboard

TAKEOFF When a surfer paddles into a wave and the ride begins

WAHINE A Hawaiian word for a girl surfer

WIPEOUT When you fall off your surfboard

WHICH MEMBER OF TEAM COUSTEAU ARE YOU?

Academy president Regina Hightower divides recruits into teams named after famous explorers. Cruz, Emmett, Bryndis, and Sailor are all members of Team Cousteau, named after the French explorer, filmmaker, and marine conservationist Jacques-Yves Cousteau.

Circle an answer to each question below. When you are finished, add up your score to discover which Explorer Academy recruit you have the most in common with.

1 Choose a favorite tool for your expedition.
a. a mind-reading baseball cap
b. rock climbing gear
c. a microscope
d. a camera

2 Which ancient civilization interests you the most?
a. Roman
b. Egypt
c. Viking
d. Aztec

3 Which obstacle course event are you the best at?
a. figuring out how to avoid the obstacle course
b. hurdles
c. cargo net
d. rock wall

4 You're in a CAVE simulation and a swarm of bats flies toward your group. What do you do?
a. try to confuse them with a sonic blast
b. run
c. warn your team that they're coming
d. try to snap a photo of the bats in flight

5 Which class is your favorite?
a. biology
b. survival training
c. anthropology
d. journalism

6 Where are you most eager to explore?
a. somewhere with an amazing library
b. anywhere sunny and warm
c. anywhere near water
d. everywhere

7 What's your favorite room in the Academy?
a. the cafeteria
b. the museum
c. the planetarium
d. the CAVE simulator

8 Which word best describes you?
a. creative
b. athletic
c. observant
d. fearless

9 What's your favorite way to travel?
a. car
b. train
c. plane
d. ship

10 Which expression do you use most?
a. Are you going to eat that?
b. Sweet as!
c. Are you okay?
d. Let's do it!

ADD UP YOUR SCORE!

A = 1   B = 2   C = 3   D = 4

YOUR SCORE =

CAVE
IS THE ACRONYM FOR COMPUTER ANIMATED VIRTUAL EXPERIENCE, A LARGE ROOM IN THE BASEMENT OF EXPLORER ACADEMY WHERE STUDENTS SIMULATE TRAINING MISSIONS.

10-15 POINTS

You're like Emmett!

Emmett is a tech whiz and a creative thinker who invents the tools he needs to solve problems. He researches every challenge carefully so he is well prepared. Also, he's always hungry!

16-23 POINTS

You're like Sailor!

New Zealand native Sailor is athletic and competitive—but she's also very friendly and loyal to every member of her team. Sailor loves to be outside, but she hates the cold.

24-33 POINTS

You're like Bryndis!

Quiet and thoughtful, this native of Iceland is a careful observer whose skills come in handy whenever there's a mystery to solve. If Bryndis thinks that someone is being treated unfairly, she will stand up for them.

34-40 POINTS

You're like Cruz!

Cruz is chill and easygoing, but don't let his laid-back demeanor fool you. He is eager to be an explorer and will work hard to achieve his dreams. Cruz is not afraid to look danger in the face when he's in trouble, and he'll take risks to protect his friends and discover the secrets that his mother left behind.

x

z

ALOHA,
HAWAII!

All the listed words describe things you can see or do in Cruz's home state of Hawaii. Can you fit them all in the grid? Place words horizontally or vertically, one letter per box.

3 LETTERS
LEI
SUN

4 LETTERS
BAYS
HULA
LUAU
MAUI
OAHU

5 LETTERS
KAUAI
LANAI
MAILI
OCEAN
SCUBA

6 LETTERS
ATOLLS
NIIHAU
WAILEA

7 LETTERS
BEACHES
ISLANDS
KILAUEA
MOLOKAI
WAIKIKI

8 LETTERS
HONOLULU

9 LETTERS
KAHOOLAWE
POLYNESIA

11 LETTERS
NA PALI COAST

THE
HAWAIIAN LANGUAGE
USES ONLY
12 LETTERS
IN ITS ALPHABET: THE VOWELS A, E, I, O, U, AND THE CONSONANTS H, K, L, M, N, P, W.

PIXEL *SURFBOARD*

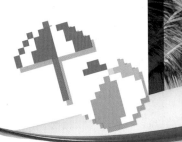

Every surfer needs an awesome surfboard. Use the key to color in each square. Or choose your own colors, as long as you pick a different color for each number! Then compare your pixel surfboard to the finished one in the back of the book.

5	5	5	5	5	5	5	5	5	5	5	5	5	5	5	5	5	5	5	5	5	5	5	5
5	5	5	4	4	4	3	5	5	5	5	5	5	5	5	5	5	5	5	5	5	5	5	5
5	5	4	6	4	4	4	3	5	5	5	5	5	5	5	5	5	5	5	5	5	5	5	5
5	5	6	6	6	4	4	4	3	5	5	5	5	5	5	5	5	5	5	5	5	5	5	5
5	5	4	4	6	6	4	4	4	3	5	5	5	5	5	5	5	5	5	5	5	5	5	5
5	5	2	4	4	6	6	4	4	4	3	5	5	5	5	5	5	5	5	5	5	5	5	5
5	5	2	2	4	4	6	6	4	4	4	3	5	5	5	5	5	5	5	5	5	5	5	5
5	5	5	2	4	4	4	6	6	4	4	4	3	5	5	5	5	5	5	5	5	5	5	5
5	5	5	5	2	2	4	4	6	6	4	4	4	3	5	5	5	5	5	5	5	5	5	5
5	5	5	5	5	2	2	4	4	6	6	4	4	4	3	5	5	5	5	5	5	5	5	5
5	5	5	5	5	5	2	4	4	4	6	6	4	4	4	3	5	5	5	5	5	5	5	5
5	5	5	5	5	5	5	2	2	4	4	4	6	6	4	4	4	3	5	5	5	5	5	5
5	5	5	5	5	5	5	5	2	2	4	4	4	6	6	4	4	4	3	5	5	5	5	5
5	5	5	5	5	5	5	5	5	2	2	4	4	4	6	6	4	4	3	5	5	5	5	5
5	5	5	5	5	5	5	5	5	5	2	2	4	4	4	6	6	4	4	3	5	5	5	5
5	5	5	5	5	5	5	5	5	5	5	2	2	4	4	4	6	6	4	4	3	5	5	5
5	5	5	5	5	5	5	5	5	5	5	5	2	2	4	4	4	6	6	4	4	5	5	5
5	5	5	5	5	5	5	5	5	5	5	5	5	2	2	4	4	4	6	1	1	5	5	5
5	5	5	5	5	5	5	5	5	5	5	5	5	5	2	2	2	4	1	5	5	5	5	5
5	5	5	5	5	5	5	5	5	5	5	5	5	5	5	5	2	4	1	5	5	5	5	5
5	5	5	5	5	5	5	5	5	5	5	5	5	5	5	5	5	5	5	5	5	5	5	5

COLOR KEY

BLUE = 1   YELLOW = 4
RED = 2   SKY BLUE = 5
GREEN = 3   ORANGE = 6

THE **ADVENTURE** *BEGINS* ›

ASTRONAUTS ONCE WALKED ON THE LAVA OF HAWAII'S MAUNA LOA **VOLCANO** AS A WAY TO PRACTICE EXPLORING THE MOON'S SURFACE.

Cruz is in his bedroom in Hawaii, packing to leave for Explorer Academy. Can you spot 15 differences between the picture on the left and the one on the right? Circle the ones you find.

A **MYSTERIOUS** *MESSAGE*

A Nebula agent dropped this coded message, and you found it! Use the grid to figure out which letter each two-digit number stands for. Then see if you can decode the message.

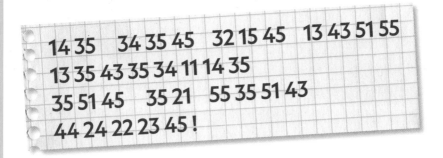

14 35   34 35 45   32 15 45   13 43 51 55
13 35 43 35 34 11 14 35
35 51 45   35 21   55 35 51 43
44 24 22 23 45 !

USE THIS GRID

	1	2	3	4	5
1	A	B	C	D	E
2	F	G	H	I	J
3	K	L	M	N	O
4	P	Q	R	S	T
5	U	V	W	X	Y/Z

ANSWER

Do not let
cruz coronado
coronado out
of your
sight

// TIP FROM CRUZ //

This type of cipher is called a Polybius square. To encrypt a letter, you replace it with the coordinates of the row and then the column in which it appears. So, for example, to encrypt the letter D, you'd use 14. To decrypt a word or a message, you use the coordinates to find each letter in the grid. So the combination 13 43 51 55 would be CRUZ.

ON THE RUN

You are being chased by a Nebula agent through the winding hallways in the basement of the Academy! How fast can you get out? Time yourself as you make your way from one end of the maze to another!

START

FINISH

START TIME	END TIME	TOTAL TIME
:	:	:

FIND THE
SPY!

EARLY MAPMAKERS ADDED MADE-UP PLACES CALLED **"PAPER TOWNS"** TO THEIR MAPS AS A WAY OF CATCHING WOULD-BE COPYCATS AND FORGERS.

There's a Nebula agent hiding out on the Explorer Academy campus. Where is he? Use the clues—and this campus map—to pinpoint his location.

CLUES

1 The spy is hiding somewhere **northward** of the Franklin Library.

2 The spy is hiding somewhere **northeast** of Bingham Auditorium.

3 The spy is hiding in a building that is **smaller** than the CAVE.

4 The spy is hiding in a building that **has a curved side.**

5 The spy is hiding in a building that is **bordered** by more than one tree.

The spy is hiding in ___The_____museum_____.

ANSWER

// TIP FROM EMMETT //

When you're solving a logic puzzle, eliminate the options that don't fit the rules at each step. That way, you can narrow down the possibilities until you're only left with one.

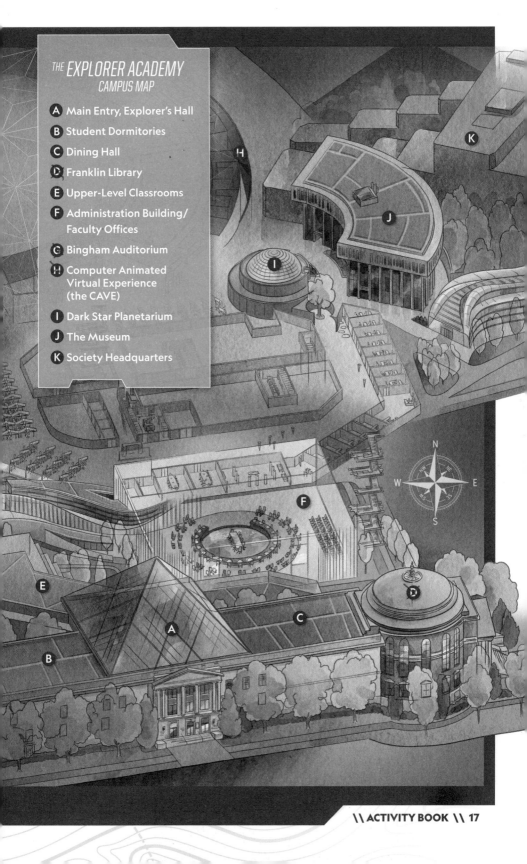

THE EXPLORER ACADEMY
CAMPUS MAP

A Main Entry, Explorer's Hall
B Student Dormitories
C Dining Hall
D Franklin Library
E Upper-Level Classrooms
F Administration Building/
   Faculty Offices
G Bingham Auditorium
H Computer Animated
   Virtual Experience
   (the CAVE)
I Dark Star Planetarium
J The Museum
K Society Headquarters

INVENT WITH EMMETT

Emmett has a lot of great ideas for inventions. For example, his eyeglasses change their shape and color depending on his mood.

Emmett has a plan to invent other accessories and clothes that can change when you wear them. What should he invent next? Think about something new, useful, or even weird that you'd want your clothes or accessories to be able to do. Draw your invention here.

STEP ONE: START BY QUICKLY SKETCHING YOUR IDEA HERE.

STEP TWO: ADD MORE DETAIL TO VISUALIZE YOUR CONCEPT.

STEP THREE: FINALIZE YOUR CONCEPT INTO A DETAILED ILLUSTRATION AND EXPLAIN WHAT IT DOES BELOW.

EXPLORING EGYPT

Academy recruit Ali Soliman is from Egypt—an area of the world that has long been a destination for explorers. Solve the clues to fill in this crossword puzzle with the names of places and things you'll find in this country filled with tombs and treasures.

ACROSS

1. Ceremonially preserved body that's wrapped in bandages
3. Giant monument with a woman's head and a lion's body
5. The sea to the east of Egypt, named after a color, is the ___ Sea.
6. A symbol similar to a cross with a loop on top, used as a symbol of life
8. A large beetle that was sacred in ancient Egypt
9. This city is the capital of Egypt.
10. Ancient Egyptian ruler
12. Watering spot in the middle of a desert
13. River that flows through Egypt and is the longest river in the world
14. Type of cloth used for a preserved body's bandages
15. A very old artifact
16. A famous boy king of Egypt, discovered in a tomb in 1922

DOWN

2. The sea to the north of Egypt is called the ___ Sea.
3. The vast North African desert that extends into Egypt is called the ___.
4. A large underground vault where the dead are buried
5. A name shared by many famous pharaohs, including one known as "the Great"
6. Somebody who digs things up to study history
7. The ancient Egyptians used sheets of this instead of paper.
11. A building devoted to the worship of a god or gods
12. A tall stone pillar that narrows at the top, as found at some ancient Egyptian sites

EXPERTS BELIEVE IT TOOK BUILDERS **20 YEARS** TO ASSEMBLE THE GREAT PYRAMID OF GIZA'S ESTIMATED **2.3 MILLION STONES.**

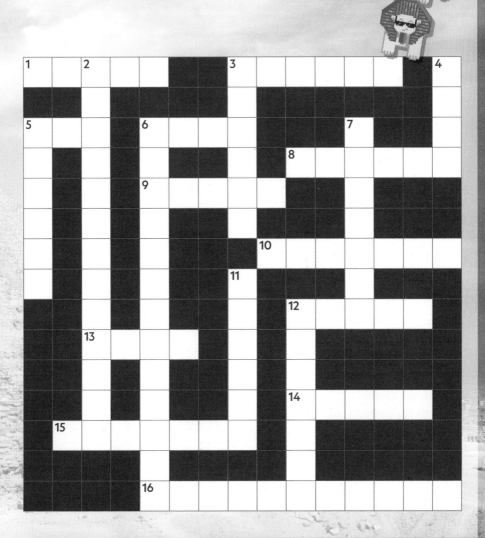

WORD BANK

Here are the entries you'll need to place in the grid—it's up to you to figure out which entry goes with which clue!

ANKH
ANTIQUE
ARCHAEOLOGIST
CAIRO
LINEN

MEDITERRANEAN
MUMMY
NILE
OASIS
OBELISK

PAPYRUS
PHARAOH
RAMSES
RED
SAHARA

SCARAB
SPHINX
TEMPLE
TOMB
TUTANKHAMUN

HIDDEN
RELICS ▶

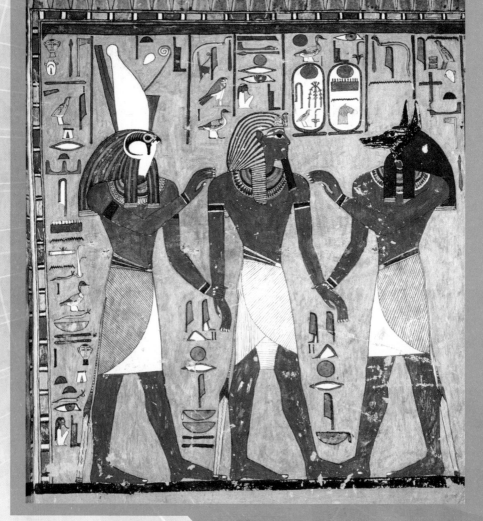

Cruz's aunt Marisol teaches archaeology at the Academy. She's showing the recruits images from a pharaoh's tomb that she excavated—but the picture on the right has 15 differences from the one on the left. Can you spot them all? Circle the ones you find.

NO CAVITIES?
THANK THE EGYPTIANS. THEY INVENTED **TOOTHPASTE!**

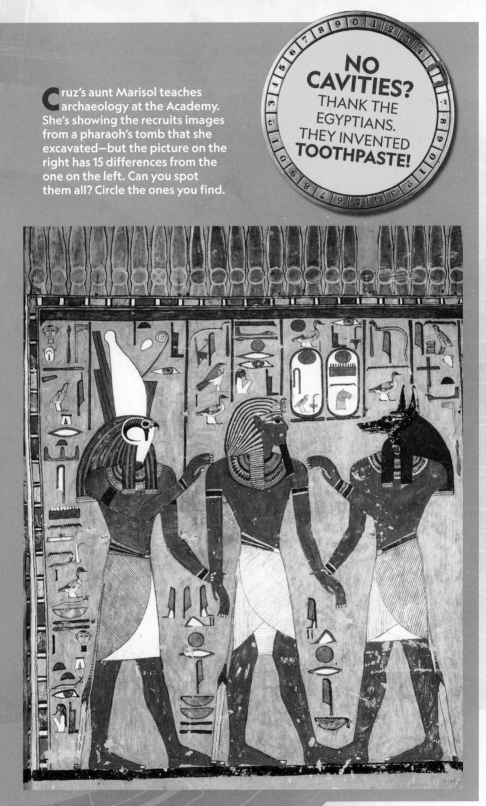

ALL ABOARD *ORION*!

This passenger ship is the flagship expedition vessel of the Explorer Academy fleet. You'll have a better chance of finding your way around if you can unscramble the names of each area of the ship. Note: The spaces between words are there just to confuse you!

SO GREAT	SLAB
VAIN MICE	NO GLUE
I AM RUT	MR COOL OR NOT
BRICK-EDGED	US CAB
NICE BOOK ADVERTS	BIG RED
MASS COLORS	ICY BASK
LAY GEL	FLUFFY ICE COATS

WORD BANK

ATRIUM	CONTROL ROOM	LOUNGE	SICK BAY
BRIDGE	FACULTY OFFICES	MINI CAVE	STORAGE
BRIDGE DECK	GALLEY	OBSERVATION DECK	
CLASSROOMS	LABS	SCUBA	

LAND HO!

Can you transform the word BOAT into the word LAND? Change one letter of the word each time to form a new, real word. Use the clues to help you.

1. *BOAT*

2. *To move or run away suddenly*

3. *Being confident and courageous*

4. *Lacking hair on one's head*

5. *Musicians who play together*

6. *LAND*

BOAT

LAND

FIND THE *FISH*

Orion has stopped so that you can explore a coral reef. Professor Ishikawa, who teaches biology and oceanography, has instructed you to find the humphead wrasse—a reef-dwelling fish with a bulge in its forehead that can grow longer than six feet (1.8 m)! Snorkel through the maze until you find it.

START

FINISH

START TIME

END TIME

TOTAL TIME

DESIGN A SHIP

What kind of ship would you use to travel around the world and explore different terrains, animals, and cultures? Design it here. Think about all the different types of rooms and the tools you would need for your expedition.

NUMBER *CRUNCHING*

Puzzles like sudoku are a great way to keep your brain sharp and boost working memory—skills you need to stay in the top of the class at Explorer Academy.

To solve this puzzle, fill in all of the empty squares so that the numbers 1 through 6 appear only once in each row, column, and box.

5			2		
1					6
		1			
				4	
	5				6
		2			3

START TIME ☐☐:☐☐   END TIME ☐☐:☐☐   TOTAL TIME ☐☐:☐☐

WORD *PLAY*

Every square, row, and column in this puzzle must contain one of each letter in the word SLEUTH. If you complete the puzzle correctly, the letters in the diagonal squares will spell out a word that means "to move quickly."

	S		E		
T					
E			L		
		H			S
					H
		U		T	

TIME IT! SEE HOW LONG IT TAKES YOU TO COMPLETE BOTH PUZZLES. THERE WILL BE OTHER SUDOKU AND LETTER SUDOKU PUZZLES LATER IN THE BOOK. CAN YOU IMPROVE YOUR TIME IN THE NEXT ROUND?

START TIME ☐☐:☐☐   END TIME ☐☐:☐☐   TOTAL TIME ☐☐:☐☐

WHO'S
WHO?

Can you find the names of Cruz's friends and family and more hidden in this puzzle? Look up, down, backward, and diagonally, and circle the names you find.

```
E T L E N A Z W B A I F S N W
E D L O D H A U D S F T D R D
S R E M S H Z H R I S R Z R S
S L I S S I E T L C I M G L H
K E R N A L R C T S I A N N M
O G E M I I E A H E B I L I S
O R U C T S L I M R M I Y D I
R A Y R N I K O I T N M O U D
R N R Y I A T E R A N B E G N
M D R L W D L A L A S U L A Y
S A R A T D R A D U Z M A N R
T D D R B E N E D I C T I M B
H U B B A R D O R C I A N C I
W R A I D O M R D I Z T Y Y A
J E R I C H O M I L E S B E E
```

AUNT MARISOL
BRYNDIS
CRUZ
DR. BENEDICT
DR. GABRIEL
DR. ISHIKAWA
DR. LEGRAND
DR. MODI
DUGAN
EMMETT
HUBBARD
JERICHO MILES
LANI
MR. ROOK
RENSHAW
SAILOR
TARYN SECLIFF
ZANE

PLOT *YOUR* ADVENTURE

You are about to embark on an ocean adventure. Which countries will you visit? Use the map to figure out where your journey will take you.

ITINERARY

1 Begin your journey in Cruz's home state, Hawaii. Travel due east until you reach this country, bordered by the United States in the north.

ANSWER

2 Travel south around the bottom of South America and head north. Then stop in the country that is bordered by the Atlantic Ocean to the east and Peru to the west.

ANSWER

3 Head north until you reach this island, located southeast of Greenland and west of Norway. Hint: Bryndis is from this country.

ANSWER

4 Now set a course for Africa. Go south and stop in this coastal country bordered by Nigeria and Gabon.

ANSWER

5 Your next mission takes you to an African island off the coast of Mozambique.

ANSWER

6 Travel north and east to this country, which is bordered by Pakistan and Bangladesh.

ANSWER

7 Then head southeast and down under, to the only country that is also a continent.

ANSWER

8 End your journey by traveling north to this island nation east of South Korea. Celebrate a job well done with a tray of sushi!

ANSWER

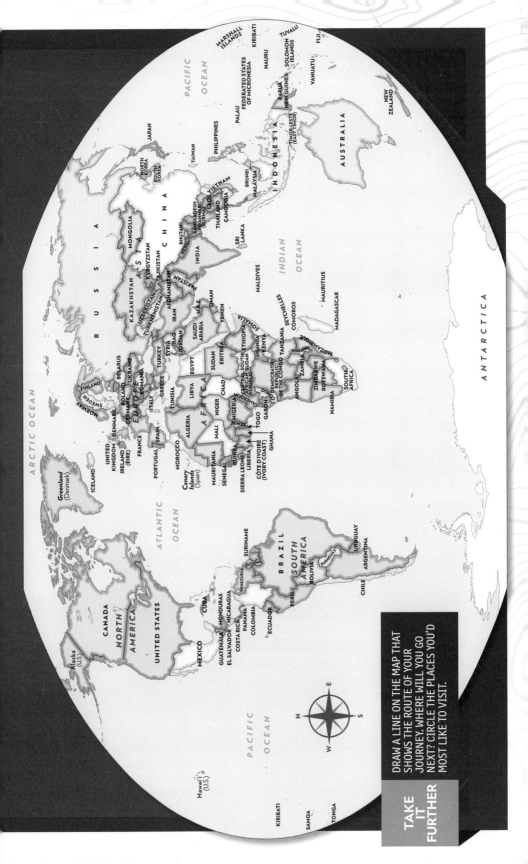

TAKE IT FURTHER

DRAW A LINE ON THE MAP THAT SHOWS THE ROUTE OF YOUR JOURNEY. WHERE WILL YOU GO NEXT? CIRCLE THE PLACES YOU'D MOST LIKE TO VISIT.

GEAR UP FOR
ICELAND

Team Cousteau member Bryndis Jónsdóttir is from Iceland. She needs to get ready for an expedition in her home country, where she'll be ice climbing, traveling across snowy plains, and whale watching. Color Bryndis in and draw all of the gear she will need for her adventure.

// TIP FROM BRYNDIS //

Climbers wear glacier glasses to protect their eyes from the light reflecting off the ice. A helmet, waterproof boots, an ice ax, and climbing harness are some other types of gear ice climbers use.

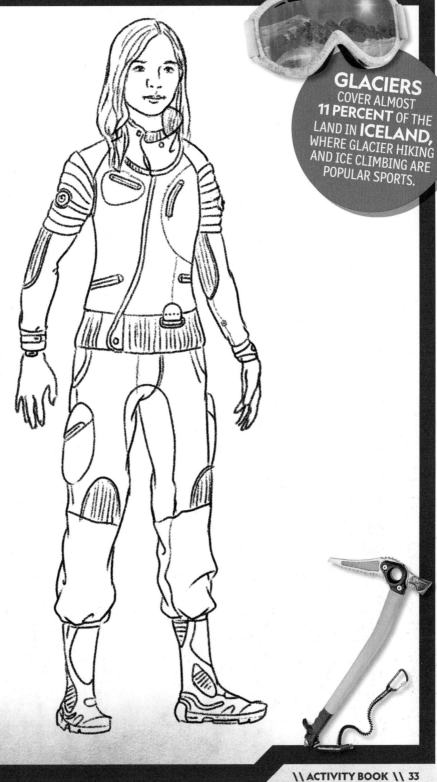

GLACIERS COVER ALMOST **11 PERCENT** OF THE LAND IN **ICELAND,** WHERE GLACIER HIKING AND ICE CLIMBING ARE POPULAR SPORTS.

BUNDLE UP
AND GET
MOVING

All of these words are things you'll find and do when it's cold outside, like when you're hanging out in Iceland with Bryndis. Can you fit them all in the grid? Place words horizontally or vertically, one letter per box.

3 LETTERS
ICE

4 LETTERS
COLD
GALE
LUGE
SNOW

5 LETTERS
BRISK
SLEDS
SLEET

6 LETTERS
CHILLY
FREEZE
GLOVES
SKIING

7 LETTERS
ICICLES
SNOWMAN

8 LETTERS
BLIZZARD
SNOWBALL
TOBOGGAN
WHITEOUT

10 LETTERS
ICE FISHING
SNOWFLAKES
SNOWMOBILE

LAND OF ICE AND SNOW

Hidden in this word search puzzle are the names of some of the natural and historical wonders you can encounter in Iceland. Circle the ones you can find. In order to make this word search more challenging, we've left the accent marks off of Langjökull and Reykjavík.

```
O I E P R G S R G S G N A S S
W B S S G N I R P S T O H T N
A L R K R E F J O R D S H G I
T A E I S R E S Y E G G L L L
E C I V K D S F Y E I L L A V
R K C A R B L A E L O U K O O
F S A J J E L E N Y K E L S P
A A L K A S E R I O S C E U A
L N G Y D O E D J F A Y F N K
L D E E G H K G N N A F L R P
S T S R T C N O O I I V N E S
L E S R K A J E R N E O A E U
N E O R L L S R S I R R V L R
F N T H E B L U E L A G O O N
G H N L K S S O F L L U G R F
```

BLACK SAND
FJORDS
GEYSERS
GLACIERS
GULLFOSS
HOT SPRINGS
LAKES
LANGJOKULL
LAVA FIELDS
NORTHERN LIGHTS
PUFFINS
REINDEER
REYKJAVIK
THE BLUE LAGOON
VOLCANOES
WATERFALLS

HEKLA AND KRAFLA ARE TWO OF MORE THAN **150** OF ICELAND'S **VOLCANOES.** ICELAND SITS ON TOP OF TWO **TECTONIC PLATES—** MASSIVE SLABS OF ROCK UNDER THE OCEAN.

y

CAVE
CONUNDRUM

b

d

f

h

j

n

p

r

t

z

Y ou are on a mission with your team in Iceland, exploring the ice caves inside a glacier, when you become separated from your teammates. Can you find them again?

(MAZE)

START

FINISH

THE **EXPLORERS'** *MOTTO*

The motto of Explorer Academy is etched in marble across its entrance. Before you can enter, you need to decode the cipher and recite the motto. To solve this cipher, write the letters in the specified columns in the grid. Then read the grid's rows from left to right (starting at row 1) to discover the motto.

EXAMPLE

To reveal the hidden motto, you must copy each row of letters into its matching column in the empty table at the right. For example, if you had:

- **COLUMN 1:** L E I
- **COLUMN 2:** I T S
- **COLUMN 3:** K H [BLANK]

you would copy them into the columns like this: ⟶

	COLUMNS		
ROWS	**1**	**2**	**3**
1	L	I	K
2	E	T	H
3	I	S	

Now read the hidden message left to right, starting at row 1 and working your way down. They spell out, from top to bottom, "LIKETHIS." It's up to you to figure out where the spaces should go; in this case, the hidden message is "LIKE THIS."

PUZZLE

Try it yourself, using the following columns:

- **COLUMN 1:** T C T O T T
- **COLUMN 2:** O O O V O E
- **COLUMN 3:** D V I A P C
- **COLUMN 4:** I E N T R T
- **COLUMN 5:** S R N E O [BLANK]

ANSWER

	1	2	3	4	5
1					
2					
3					
4					
5					
6					

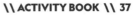

WHICH SUBJECT
WOULD YOU TEACH AT THE ACADEMY?

Maybe one day you'd like to take a break from exploring and teach at the Academy. Which subject would you focus on? Circle your answer to each question. Then add up your score at the end to discover which class you'd be most likely to teach.

1 What relaxes you?
a. getting your hands dirty
b. going on a five-mile (8-km) run
c. swimming
d. reading a good book

2 Which book would you take off the shelf?
a. *Exploring the Ancient Tomb*
b. *Lost in the Jungle*
c. *Journey of the Blue Whale*
d. *Breaking the Unbreakable Code*

3 Choose a snack:
a. aged cheddar
b. trail mix
c. sushi
d. alphabet soup

4 What's your favorite season?
a. spring
b. winter
c. summer
d. fall

5 Your friends think you are ...
a. curious
b. tough
c. caring
d. clever

6 You'd like to volunteer to:
a. help out on an archaeological dig
b. save an endangered species
c. pick up litter on a beach
d. tutor kids in reading

7 If you weren't a teacher, you'd be:
a. a museum guide
b. a camp counselor
c. a lifeguard
d. a mystery writer

8 What sound makes you happy?
a. classical music
b. nature sounds
c. dolphin calls
d. the tapping of Morse code

9 What do you like to do on a rainy afternoon?
a. watch a documentary about ancient Greece
b. go on a mud run
c. meditate to the peaceful sound of the raindrops
d. finish a bunch of crossword puzzles

10 Your most useful item of clothing or accessory is:
a. a vest to hold all of your tools
b. hiking boots
c. a wet suit
d. a pair of dark sunglasses

ADD UP YOUR SCORE!

A = 1   B = 2   C = 3   D = 4

YOUR SCORE =

10-14 POINTS

Archaeology

You love learning about the past and dream of traveling around the world and visiting the sites of ancient civilizations. After studying the subject yourself, you'd make a great archaeology professor!

15-22 POINTS

Survival Training

You would rather be outdoors than indoors. You're not afraid of being outside in harsh climates, like extreme heat or extreme cold. You hope to one day live off the land. For those reasons, you'd be a great teacher of survival training.

23-32 POINTS

Oceanography

You are drawn to water and are always thinking about the ocean. You care about the health of the world's oceans and the creatures that inhabit it. Your students will learn a lot from you when you teach them oceanography!

34-40 POINTS

Cryptology

Your love of words and reading has led to a love of codes and ciphers. You have fun solving puzzles and mysteries. You'll enjoy being a cryptology teacher at the Academy—and coming up with ciphers for your students to solve!

COLORFUL *MOOD*

What mood is Emmett in today? Use the key to color in his emoto-glasses to find out.

COLOR KEY BLACK = ╱ RED = •• ORANGE = :

MOOD KEY

Orange and Red = Angry
Yellow = Happy
Bright Pink = Honest

INCREDIBLE **EXPLORERS**

Academy recruits are following in the footsteps of other explorers—men and women who traveled the world to gain knowledge about cultures and creatures they had never encountered before. Can you find the names of these famous explorers hidden in this puzzle? Look up, down, backward, and diagonally. Circle the names you find.

```
N A M S A T A Z O D N E M O M
O U C S N E S D N U M A M P L
T V Y S I E V E S P U C C I G
E S R O D R A K E A B N U M L
L N A O S N K A U L D L S N I
K S L N O S S K I R E S Y A V
C C L R E N S A I H I A N L I
A O I E O T O B N C C T U L N
H T H S A L E O O G R C H E G
S T N N O L S L C N O G U G S
N E L P L H U N E O I M S A T
H E Y T K M M I K E A H E M O
Y M E L B N B O L V D R E S N
G A O U O S A A A H O L P G E
U M S R T N R E A Y I S M N O
```

AMUNDSEN
BELL
BIRD
BLY
COOK
DRAKE
ERIKSSON
GOMES
HENSON
HILLARY
LIVINGSTONE
MAGELLAN
MENDOZA
POLO
RALEIGH
SCOTT
SHACKLETON
STANLEY
TASMAN
VESPUCCI

ANNIE LONDONDERRY WAS THE **FIRST WOMAN** TO TRAVEL AROUND THE WORLD— **ON A BICYCLE!** SHE SPENT **15 MONTHS** CYCLING AROUND THE U.S., EUROPE, AND ASIA.

SURVIVAL TRAINING

It's time to report to Rock Creek Park, where Dr. Legrand—professor of fitness and survival training at the Academy—has a survival test for you. This obstacle course contains a hurdle, monkey bars, and a cargo net. How fast can you get through it?

HURDLE

START

FINISH

START

MONKEY BARS

FINISH

IN 2018, CLIMBERS ALEX HONNOLD AND TOMMY CALDWELL SCALED THE **3,000-FOOT** (914-M) NOSE ROUTE OF YOSEMITE NATIONAL PARK'S **EL CAPITAN** IN A RECORD-BREAKING 1 HOUR, 58 MINUTES, AND 7 SECONDS.

CARGO NET

START

FINISH

WHAT'S THE WORD?

D r. Benedict teaches journalism at the Academy, and tomorrow, you've got a big test in her class. Solve this word puzzle to get your brain ready! Start at the top of the pyramid and fill in the word below it. The new word must contain all of the letters of the word above it, plus an extra letter. Keep going until you get to the bottom.

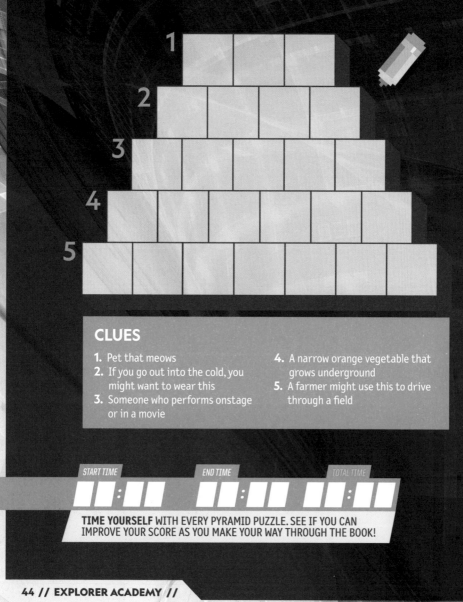

CLUES

1. Pet that meows
2. If you go out into the cold, you might want to wear this
3. Someone who performs onstage or in a movie
4. A narrow orange vegetable that grows underground
5. A farmer might use this to drive through a field

START TIME   END TIME   TOTAL TIME

TIME YOURSELF WITH EVERY PYRAMID PUZZLE. SEE IF YOU CAN IMPROVE YOUR SCORE AS YOU MAKE YOUR WAY THROUGH THE BOOK!

MIGRATING *MARVELS*

Most of the shapes in this picture contain a number. Color them in using the number-to-color key to reveal some colorful insect explorers. (Hint: Team Cousteau encountered them in a CAVE exercise designed by Dr. Gabriel, professor of conservation at the Academy.) When you're done coloring, unscramble the letters at the bottom of the page to name this creature.

COLOR KEY   ORANGE = 1   BLACK = 2   LIGHT BLUE = 3   DARK BLUE = 4

UNSCRAMBLE: **RNOMAHC EFTBISETURL**

ANSWER

ANCIENT
EXPEDITION

You are hiking around the ruins of the ancient city of Chichen Itza, Mexico, when you receive a coded message in which every pair of touching letters has been swapped. Use the key to decode it—and then decide what your next move will be!

Take a look at this example to see how it works. The original message is shown at the top, and the coded message is beneath. To make the coded message, swap each letter with the one that immediately follows it in the message.

SWAP EVERY PAIR OF LETTERS
WSPA VEREP YIAO RL FTETESR

To get back to the original message again, you just swap the letters back

WSPA VEREP YIAO RL FTETESR
SWAP EVERY PAIR OF LETTERS

DECODE THE FOLLOWING MESSAGE:

EMTE TA HTE EC LSAITLLP ORYMADI TA IMNDGITH

ANSWER Meet at the ce slialtpl

EXPLORE MEXICO

Cruz and his team have been assigned to Mexico. There are so many places to go and things to do in this country! Circle the names of these places and things hidden in this puzzle. Look up, down, backward, and diagonally.

THE **NATIONAL SYMBOL** OF MEXICO IS THE **GOLDEN EAGLE,** THE LARGEST **BIRD OF PREY** IN NORTH AMERICA.

```
E Y L C C A N C U N P U E C Z
B A P A Q A N S E G S I N N Z
N A A Y Z U A A N N C L O R Q
L S J T R N E I S O O I I U H
K Y E A A A L T R I H T I N S
U C T U C E M T Z C T N E N I
S N G I K A E I A A T A A S N
O I I R C S L I D A L X O T A
M C O Y N O R I N S O S A C P
A N E O U A C A F L A N X C S
S Y A L M C R I O O C Y A H U
A O A H O O A T X I R A C L A
S O T M O T L T Q E S N A I K
R A O N A S S Z A C M I I C S
C T T C H I C H E N I T Z A M
```

AXOLOTLS
AZTECS
BAJA CALIFORNIA
CANCUN
CENOTES
CHICHEN ITZA
COATIS
CORTES
IGUANAS
MARIACHI
MAYA
MEXICO CITY
OAXACA
OCELOTS
PYRAMIDS
QUETZALS
QUINTANA ROO
SNORKELING
SPANISH
YUCATAN

// TIP FROM EMMETT //

A cenote (pronounced sen-OH-tay) is an underground sinkhole filled with water. There are more than 5,000 of them in Mexico's Yucatan Peninsula.

DESIGN A
DORM ROOM

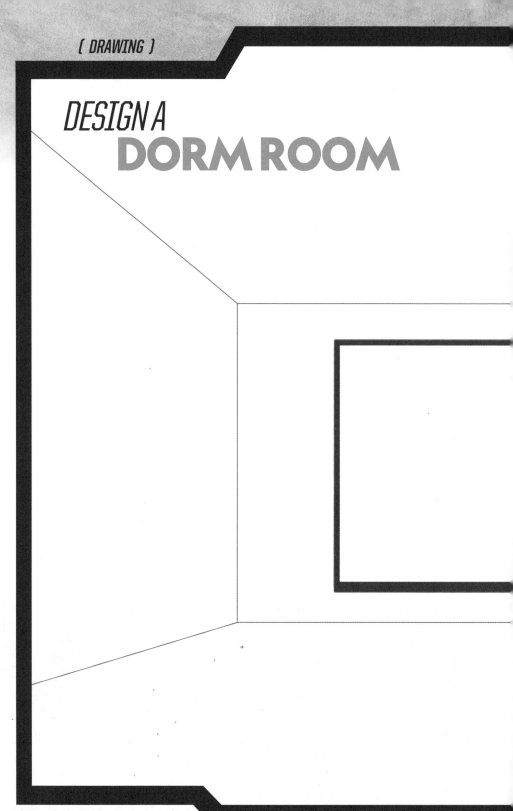

Every recruit at the Academy shares a dorm room with a roommate. What would your dream room look like? Start out by filling in the screen with a place you'd like to explore. (In Cruz's room, it's 24-hour live footage of Mount Everest.) Then add furniture, equipment, and any other gear you'll need to make your dorm room the perfect explorer headquarters!

WAVE THE FLAG

Where is your next mission, recruit? Solve this symbol code to find out! This code, called semaphore, was used by sailors at sea to communicate with people on other ships who were too far away to hear them. The sailors held two flags that they moved to different positions to represent different letters of the alphabet.

SAILORS CAME UP WITH **SHORTCUTS** FOR THE NAUTICAL FLAGS. FOR EXAMPLE, IF YOU HELD UP **THE "O" FLAG, THAT MEANT "MAN OVERBOARD!"**

DECODE THE SYMBOL CODE:

T h e   S a h h

WATCH *THE* CLOCK

Semaphore traditionally uses flags, but you don't actually need the flags: You just need some way to point in two directions at once, such as the face of a clock. The minute and hour hands of a clock can represent all the letters of the semaphore alphabet, just as if they were the arms of a person.

For example, the clock to the right, showing 3:30, represents the letter F because the hands of the clock are in roughly the same position as the arms of someone making the letter F in flag semaphore.

DECODE THE FOLLOWING TO FIND OUT WHAT SUMMER TEMPERATURES CAN REACH IN YOUR UPCOMING DESTINATION.

ANIMALS OF THE SAHARA

Life in the Sahara can be harsh. The animals that live there have adapted to survive in a land with extreme heat and scarce water. Use the clues to fill in the crossword puzzle with the names of these amazing Saharan animals.

ACROSS

2. This tall bird lies low and stretches its neck along the ground to hide from danger.
5. Book and movie, *Fantastic Mr.* ___
6. This creature carries its house on its back and leaves a slimy trail.
7. A type of monkey with a long snout and large teeth
10. Long-eared, rabbit-like animal
11. Animal that is famous for "laughing"
14. Venomous snake with large hinged fangs
15. Eight-legged creature with lobster-like pincers and a venomous sting in its tail
17. Small, fawn-colored antelope

DOWN

1. Color-changing lizard
2. Bird of prey with a distinctive hoot
3. Tailless amphibian with dry, warty skin
4. Venomous snake that can spread a hood around its neck
5. Amphibian famous for jumping from place to place
8. Alligator relative
9. Woolly animal that lives in mountainous parts of the Sahara
11. Nocturnal mammal, with a spiky coat, that can roll into a ball
12. Large black bird related to the crow
13. Burrowing, mouse-like rodent sometimes kept as a pet
16. Animal with a hump on its back, known as the "horse" of the desert

THE SAHARA IS NOT THE WORLD'S LARGEST DESERT. THAT HONOR GOES TO THE CONTINENT OF ANTARCTICA!

WORD BANK

Here are the entries you'll need to place in the grid—it's up to you to figure out which entry goes with which clue!

3 LETTERS
FOX
OWL

4 LETTERS
FROG
HARE
TOAD

5 LETTERS
CAMEL
COBRA
HYENA
RAVEN
SHEEP
SNAIL
VIPER

6 LETTERS
BABOON
GERBIL

7 LETTERS
GAZELLE
OSTRICH

8 LETTERS
HEDGEHOG
SCORPION

9 LETTERS
CHAMELEON
CROCODILE

IN THE LIBRARY ▸

Every good explorer knows that when you're in a library, you can explore the world without leaving the building. These two images of Cruz and his dad in the Academy library with Mr. Rook may look the same, but the one on the right has 15 differences from the one on the left. Can you find and circle them all?

THE LIBRARY OF CONGRESS IN WASHINGTON, D.C., IS THE **LARGEST LIBRARY IN THE WORLD.** IT HOUSES MORE THAN **168 MILLION** ITEMS ON ABOUT 838 MILES (1,349 KM) OF BOOKSHELVES.

SURF'S UP
WITH LANI

Lani Kealoha, Cruz's best friend, is his partner in crime when it comes to exploring their island home of Kauai. Fill this Hawaiian beach with plants, animals, friends, and beach gear for Lani.

EXPERT EXPLORERS

To be an explorer, you need more than an adventurous spirit. Explorers are usually experts in a topic of science, history, or other fields that prepare them to make a difference in the world. Use the clues to fill in this crossword puzzle with different fields of study an explorer might specialize in.

ACROSS

1. The study of numbers
4. The study of elements and how they react to one another
6. The study of the human body
7. The study of ideas and thoughts
11. The study of androids and other computer-controlled machines
12. The study of animals
13. The study of matter and energy, such as heat, light, and how objects interact
14. The study of the physical properties of Earth

DOWN

1. The study of human health
2. The study of human history by excavating old remains
3. The study of the human mind
5. The study of finance
8. The study of the past
9. The study of heredity and how you relate to your family members
10. The study of how humans and animals work

WORD BANK

Here are the entries you'll need to place in the grid—it's up to you to figure out which entry goes with which clue!

7 LETTERS
ANATOMY
BIOLOGY
GEOLOGY
HISTORY
PHYSICS
ZOOLOGY

8 LETTERS
GENETICS
MEDICINE
ROBOTICS

9 LETTERS
CHEMISTRY
ECONOMICS

10 LETTERS
PHILOSOPHY
PSYCHOLOGY

11 LETTERS
ARCHAEOLOGY
MATHEMATICS

WHICH FAMOUS *EXPLORER* ARE **YOU** *MOST LIKE?*

Each team of recruits is named after a famous explorer: Magellan, Cousteau, Galileo, and Earhart. Circle your answer to each question. Then add up your score at the end to find out which of these adventurers you have the most in common with.

1 Pick one way to travel:
a. on a ship
b. on a submarine
c. using your imagination
d. on a plane

2 What is your reason for exploring?
a. to look for new opportunities
b. to learn ways to protect Earth
c. to gain knowledge
d. for the thrill of it!

3 Pick a hat:
a. Magellan's round black hat   b. Cousteau's beanie

c. Hat's aren't my thing.   d. Amelia's flight hat

4 Pick a tool for exploring:
a. a map of the world
b. a snorkel
c. a telescope
d. a compass

5 You are *not* afraid of:
a. the unknown
b. sharks
c. standing up for what you believe in
d. heights

6 Your strongest subject in school is:
a. geography
b. biology
c. math
d. gym

7 Pick a color:
a. yellow
b. turquoise
c. black
d. sky blue

8 Which of these countries interests you the most?
a. Portugal
b. France
c. Italy
d. the United States

9 You would describe yourself as:
a. interested in seeing the world
b. passionate about caring for Earth
c. curious about how the universe works
d. fearless when it comes to facing challenges

10 Pick a shape:
a. wave   b. fish

c. star   d. cloud

ADD UP YOUR SCORE!

A = 1   B = 2   C = 3   D = 4

YOUR SCORE =

10-14 POINTS

You're like
Ferdinand Magellan!

This Portuguese explorer organized the first expedition of ships to circle the globe in 1519. Like him, you love sailing the seas and dream of visiting every part of the world someday.

15-22 POINTS

You're like
Jacques Cousteau!

Born in France, Cousteau spent decades in the 20th century pioneering undersea exploration. In 1974, he formed the Cousteau Society, dedicated to conserving ocean life. Like him, you are fascinated with underwater ecosystems and passionate about keeping our oceans healthy.

23-32 POINTS

You're like
Galileo Galilei!

Galileo got into a lot of trouble in the 1500s, when he put forth the theory that Earth revolves around the sun and not the other way around. Like this Italian scholar, you are drawn to the stars and hungry for explanations about the unknown.

33-40 POINTS

You're like
Amelia Earhart!

Like this pioneering aviator, you dream of one day flying around the world! Adventurous Amelia earned her pilot's license when she was 26 years old. She broke many records with her solo flights, and opened doors for other women pilots.

WHAT'S THE
WORD?

Every year, Explorer Academy recruits compete to see who will win the North Star award. Exercise your mind with word puzzles like this one and you might have a shot at winning!

Start at the top of the pyramid and fill in the word below it. The new word must contain all of the letters of the word above it, plus an extra letter. Keep going until you get to the bottom.

THE **NORTH STAR** IS ALSO KNOWN AS **POLARIS,** BECAUSE IT APPEARS AS THE BRIGHTEST STAR IN THE SKY CLOSEST TO THE NORTH POLE.

1
2
3
4
5

CLUES

1. Say something that isn't true
2. Small piece of land surrounded by water
3. Playground item
4. Departed on a boat
5. Information about something, as in "the _____ "

START TIME

END TIME

TOTAL TIME

THE *CULPER CODE*

You are due to meet Professor Coronado at a secret location in Washington, D.C. She slipped you this coded message with instructions that you must solve to figure out where and when to meet. Use the key to crack the cipher and make your way to the rendezvous point!

To decode this secret message, replace each number with the given word. So, for example, "1 23 39 31" would be "A HIDDEN SECRET MESSAGE."

CODE: 29 6 16 26 20 35 43 11 10

Code Key

1. A
2. AFTER
3. AGENTS
4. ALL
5. APPLY
6. AT
7. BASIN
8. BEFORE
9. BLACK
10. BUILDING
11. CAPITOL
12. CARE
13. CLOTHES
14. CODE
15. COME
16. DAWN
17. DUSK
18. FOR
19. FROM
20. FRONT
21. GO
22. HAT
23. HIDDEN
24. HIDE
25. HOUSE
26. IN
27. IT
28. MAKE
29. MEET
30. MEMORIAL
31. MESSAGE
32. METRO
33. MIDDAY
34. MONUMENT
35. OF
36. OFFICE
37. PARK
38. ROOSEVELT
39. SECRET
40. SPY
41. STREET
42. TAKE
43. THE
44. TIDAL
45. TIE
46. TIME
47. TO
48. WASHINGTON
49. WEAR
50. WHITE

ANSWER

SUBTERRANEAN
EXPEDITION

Dr. Coronado has hidden seven secret messages in nooks throughout a network of underground tunnels in Washington, D.C. Can you make your way through this subterranean labyrinth, collect all seven, and then head back to the entrance?

ENTRANCE

A PUZZLE OF *PRESIDENTS*

In 1790, George Washington decided that the land along the Potomac River would be the best place for the seat of our nation's government. Since then, U.S. presidents have governed from Washington, D.C. Circle the names of these presidents hidden in the puzzle.

```
E R J R R N N E O G R A N T T
I J R E X N O S R E F F E J L
D T O S C A R T E R J O S W E
I H H O N O S N H O J E I R V
O W A S H I N G T O N L N E E
N A M U R T N E O I S O I N S
M G N N L A S X I O X S T F O
A V R I G I R N N I E H E N O
D A A A N T N N N N E O E O R
I M E O O B O C H N K O N T X
S R O L F S U O O E S V T N I
O E A O K V W S D L E E T I N
N A R C N E O C H A N R E L N
T D A R R E I A D A M S E C E
N J I Y R D O S Y D E N N E K
```

ADAMS
BUSH
CARTER
CLINTON
EISENHOWER
FORD
GRANT
HOOVER
JACKSON
JEFFERSON
JOHNSON
KENNEDY
LINCOLN
MADISON
NIXON
REAGAN
ROOSEVELT
TRUMAN
WASHINGTON
WILSON

WASHINGTON, D.C., WAS DESIGNED ON A GRID, WITH THE **U.S. CAPITOL AT THE CENTER.**

THE STREETS OF D.C.

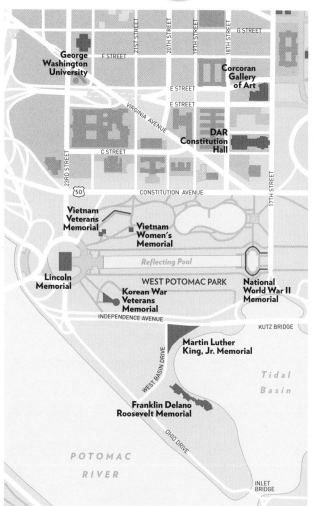

While exploring Washington, D.C., it's a good idea to get to know your surroundings. Use the map to answer the questions below—and take a tour of the nation's capital while you're at it.

CLUES

1 Start at the Washington Monument. Head north on 15th Street, then west on Constitution Avenue. What memorial do you spot just south of 17th Street?

ANSWER

2 Continue west on Constitution Avenue, then head south when you reach 23rd Street. What "presidential" memorial do you soon come upon?

ANSWER

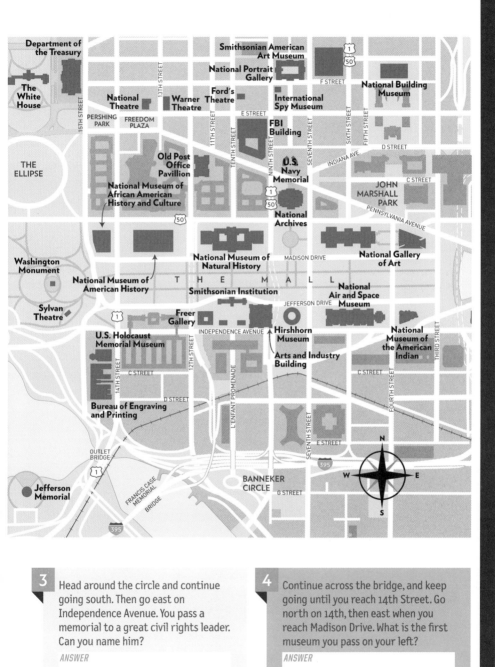

Map labels:

Department of the Treasury
Smithsonian American Art Museum
National Portrait Gallery
The White House
National Theatre
Warner Theatre
Ford's Theatre
International Spy Museum
National Building Museum
13TH STREET
F STREET
PERSHING PARK
FREEDOM PLAZA
E STREET
FBI Building
11TH STREET
TENTH STREET
NINTH STREET
SEVENTH STREET
SIXTH STREET
FIFTH STREET
D STREET
15TH STREET
THE ELLIPSE
Old Post Office Pavilion
U.S. Navy Memorial
INDIANA AVE.
JOHN MARSHALL PARK
C STREET
National Museum of African American History and Culture
National Archives
PENNSYLVANIA AVENUE
Washington Monument
National Museum of American History
National Museum of Natural History
MADISON DRIVE
National Gallery of Art
THE MALL
Smithsonian Institution
National Air and Space Museum
Sylvan Theatre
Freer Gallery
JEFFERSON DRIVE
INDEPENDENCE AVENUE
Hirshhorn Museum
National Museum of the American Indian
THIRD STREET
U.S. Holocaust Memorial Museum
14TH STREET
C STREET
12TH STREET
L'ENFANT PROMENADE
Arts and Industry Building
C STREET
FOURTH STREET
D STREET
Bureau of Engraving and Printing
SEVENTH STREET
E STREET
OUTLET BRIDGE
Jefferson Memorial
FRANCIS CASE MEMORIAL BRIDGE
BANNEKER CIRCLE
G STREET
N
W   E
S

3 Head around the circle and continue going south. Then go east on Independence Avenue. You pass a memorial to a great civil rights leader. Can you name him?

ANSWER

4 Continue across the bridge, and keep going until you reach 14th Street. Go north on 14th, then east when you reach Madison Drive. What is the first museum you pass on your left?

ANSWER

DRAW CRUZ

Follow the steps to draw a Cruz Coronado portrait using the illustration below. You'll need a sharp pencil (so keep a sharpener nearby) and a good eraser. Start by sketching lightly so you can erase your guidelines and fine-tune your final drawing in the box on the right. When you're done, color him in!

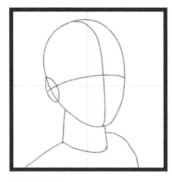

STEP ONE
Draw horizontal and vertical guidelines to help you draw the face in proportion to the original image. Lightly sketch an oval for the head and a line to show the placement of the eyes, nearly halfway down the head.

STEP TWO
Add shapes for the eyes, nose, and mouth. Don't forget the eyebrows! Lightly sketch the shape of Cruz's wavy hair.

STEP THREE
Add detail to the face with darker pencil lines. Give texture to the hair, clothing, and backpack strap by adding lines. Then sketch in Cruz's necklace.

STEP FOUR
Finalize your drawing by shading to create a sense of shape. Erase your guidelines, and add color if you like!

DRAW CRUZ HERE

// TIP FROM CRUZ //

Drawing is just like exercise—the more you do it, the better you get at it. Sketching is the warm-up, and with practice you'll be creating masterpieces of your own!

WHAT'S THE *SECRET WORD?*

Can you fill in the puzzle grid with these words about spies and secrets? Place words horizontally or vertically, one letter per box.

4 LETTERS
CLUE
CODE
DROP
MOLE
VISA

5 LETTERS
AGENT
ASSET
COVER

6 LETTERS
CIPHER
DEVICE
RIDDLE
SECRET

7 LETTERS
CLEANER
CONCEAL
HANDLER
MYSTERY
STEALTH

8 LETTERS
DEFECTOR
PASSPORT

9 LETTERS
ESPIONAGE
SPYMASTER

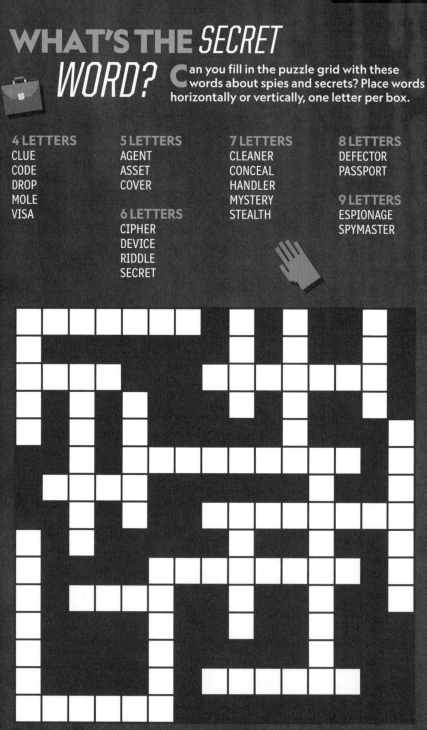

BY THE NUMBERS

Here's another pyramid puzzle ... but this time it's with numbers, not letters! Every square in the pyramid must contain a value exactly equal to the total of the two squares immediately beneath it.

THE FIRST RECORDED USE OF THE **NUMBER ZERO** WAS AROUND 3 B.C. IN **MESOPOTAMIA**, THE REGION IN SOUTHWESTERN ASIA WHERE THE EARLIEST CIVILIZATION IN THE WORLD DEVELOPED.

99

51

13   14   14

START TIME

END TIME

TOTAL TIME

HINT: START AT THE BOTTOM AND WORK YOUR WAY UP.

RAINFOREST *RESCUE*

Professor Gabriel is sending the recruits into the Amazon jungle to observe the feeding habits of squirrel monkeys. Suit up Sailor with a camouflage uniform so she can study the monkeys without being seen, and draw any equipment she'll need to survive in the jungle.

// TIP FROM SAILOR //

Think about bringing a camera and a note-book to record your observations. And remember that most rainforests get about 100 inches (254 cm) of rain a year, so think of ways to keep your gear—and yourself!—dry.

ANALS OF
NEW ZEALAND

Connect the dots to reveal two animals native to New Zealand, Sailor's home country. Unscramble the words underneath each picture to reveal the animal's name.

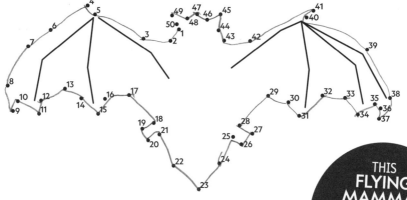

UNSCRAMBLE: **GOLN-DLTEIA TBA**

ANSWER

THIS
**FLYING
MAMMAL**
ONLY WEIGHS
LESS THAN
ONE OUNCE
(28 GRAMS).

THIS
**ENDANGERED
AMPHIBIAN**
IS A MASTER OF
CAMOUFLAGE.

UNSCRAMBLE: **'SYRAHEC GORF**

ANSWER

EXPLORE
NEW ZEALAND

Sailor's home is known for its beautiful coastline, majestic mountains, and green landscapes. It's also a popular destination for extreme sports lovers. Hidden in this puzzle are places and things to do, see, and explore in New Zealand. Look up, down, backward, and diagonally, and circle the ones you find.

```
G D R V S J H A K A M I E B D
S N E S H E E P I A O W U K N
Q U H D U N E D I N Y N M I U
U O S I H K E A H B G C O E O
E S R D I B O I G E H R U C S
E D E W N O K U E R D E N W L
N R I E K I R J I N H W T E U
S O C E N V U S A U R O V L F
T F A G O M T L M U D T I L T
O L L E P C K M C E J Y C I B
W I G I H C R A R O Y K T N U
N M N U U A V O R A W S O G O
E G R A T E N A P I E R R T D
L C L A S A U R O T O R I O O
H N R E F R E V L I S R A N T
```

AUCKLAND
BUNGEE JUMPING
CAVES
CHRISTCHURCH
DOUBTFUL SOUND
DUNEDIN
GLACIERS
HAKA
HIKING
KIWI
MILFORD SOUND
MOUNT VICTORIA
NAPIER
QUEENSTOWN
ROTORUA
RUGBY
SHEEP
SILVER FERN
SKY TOWER
WELLINGTON

WITHOUT MANY **PREDATORS** ON THE GROUND TO BOTHER THEM, THE DESCENDANTS OF **KIWIS** LOST THE ABILITY TO **FLY.**

FIORDLAND
NATIONAL PARK

One of the most beautiful destinations in New Zealand is this 2.97-million-acre (1.2-million-ha) park featuring rainforests, lakes, mountains, and fjords—inlets surrounded by cliffs on either side. Take a run through the winding trails of this park until you reach the exit. The trails cross over and under each other, using the marked bridges.

START

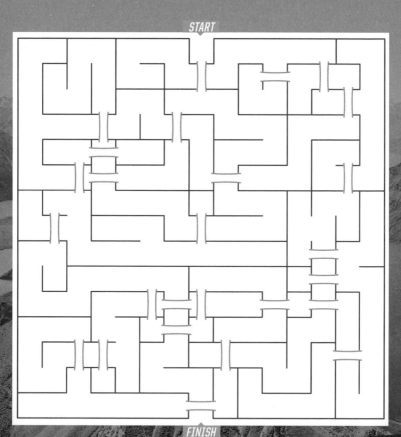

FINISH

// TIP FROM SAILOR //

The indigenous people of New Zealand are the Maori. According to their legends, the fjords were carved out by the demigod Tu-te-raki-whanoa with his adze, a type of ax.

BY THE NUMBERS

To solve this puzzle, write a number in each empty square. Every square in the pyramid must contain a value exactly equal to the total of the two squares immediately beneath it.

24	18

10			7

6	

START TIME ☐☐:☐☐ END TIME ☐☐:☐☐☐ TOTAL TIME ☐☐:☐☐

DRAW HUBBARD

Hubbard is the unofficial mascot of the Academy's recruits. He can usually be found hanging out with his owner, Taryn Secliff. Follow the steps to draw this curious canine. You'll need a sharp pencil (so keep a sharpener nearby) and a good eraser. Remember to start by sketching lightly so you can erase your guidelines and fine-tune your final drawing.

STEP ONE
Draw guidelines to help you place elements in your drawing in proportion to the original image of Hubbard. Lightly sketch a circle for the head, and shapes and lines for the body as shown. These are called gesture lines.

STEP TWO
Add basic shapes for the eyes, nose, and mouth as well as a line for Hubbard's snout. Draw in the shape of the paws.

STEP THREE
Add texture to the fur, and sketch in Hubbard's jacket and straps.

STEP FOUR
Finalize by adding more lines to the fur— some thicker, and some thinner. Add shading to create depth. Then erase your guidelines and add color in your drawing if you'd like!

DRAW HUBBARD HERE

HUBBARD IS A WEST HIGHLAND WHITE TERRIER, A BREED THAT IS MORE THAN 300 YEARS OLD AND ORIGINALLY FROM SCOTLAND. THESE PLAYFUL PUPS ARE KNOWN AS **"WESTIES"** FOR SHORT.

DESTINATION:
DUGAN'S HOMETOWN

Morse code is a method of communication that uses sounds or flashes of light of two different lengths. Short sounds or flashes are called "dots," and long sounds or flashes are called "dashes." This also makes Morse code easy to write down, since you can write the dots as a period and the dashes as a dash symbol.

YOUR NEXT DESTINATION IS THE HOMETOWN OF ACADEMY RECRUIT DUGAN MARSH.

WHERE IS HE FROM? USE THE KEY TO FIND OUT.

A	.-	B	-...	C	-.-.	D	-..	E	.	F	..-.
G	--.	H	....	I	..	J	.---	K	-.-	L	.-..
M	--	N	-.	O	---	P	.--.	Q	--.-	R	.-.
S	...	T	-	U	..-	V	...-	W	.--	X	-..-
Y	-.--	Z	--..	,	--..--						

ANSWER

... . - -. - . .-. . -..-.

-. . -- . .. . -..- .. .-.- ---

UP, UP, AND *AWAY*

Hot-air ballooning is a popular activity in New Mexico. Dr. Gabriel is giving the recruits a hands-on lesson on how hot-air balloons work. Use the key to color in this picture of a hot-air balloon.

EVERY DAY, SCIENTISTS SEND **RIDERLESS WEATHER BALLOONS** INTO THE ATMOSPHERE TO COLLECT DATA ABOUT AIR TEMPERATURE, PRESSURE, HUMIDITY, AND WIND SPEED.

COLOR KEY

RED = 1   YELLOW = 2   ORANGE = 3   GREEN = 4   LIGHT BLUE = 5
PURPLE = 6   DARK BLUE = 7

ANIMALS OF NEW MEXICO

Can you unscramble the names of these animals from New Mexico? Remember, most of the spaces between words are just there to confuse you!

1 This wild pig is also known as a peccary.

UNSCRAMBLE: **JAIL EVAN**

ANSWER

2 The short tail on this wildcat gives it its name.

UNSCRAMBLE: **TAB COB**

ANSWER

3 The body of this rodent is covered with 30,000 or more sharp quills.

UNSCRAMBLE: **UPPER COIN**

ANSWER

4 This feline predator's main source of food is deer.

UNSCRAMBLE: **A RUG CO**

ANSWER

5 This bird prefers using its legs to flying.

UNSCRAMBLE: **ORDER AN URN**

ANSWER

6 This mammal is known for its long ears and hind legs.

UNSCRAMBLE: **JAB AT BRICK**

ANSWER

7 This reptile is a venomous lizard.

UNSCRAMBLE: **MERIT SLOGAN**

ANSWER

8 This great climber is named for the large, curly protrusions from its forehead.

UNSCRAMBLE: **HE BRINGS HOPE**

ANSWER

WORD BANK

BIGHORN SHEEP
BOBCAT
COUGAR
GILA MONSTER

JACKRABBIT
JAVELINA
PORCUPINE
ROADRUNNER

TINY *TECH*

Connect the dots to reveal one of Cruz's most important gadgets.

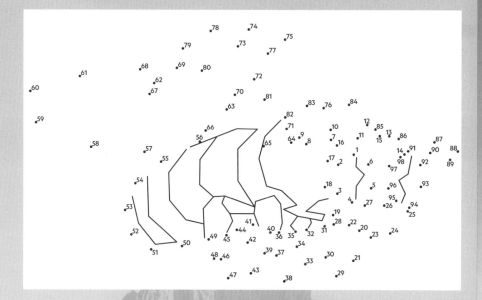

[CIPHER]

THE CLUE IN THE BOOK

Cruz's mother left him a riddle in a book that was special to both of them. Use the key to decode the name of the book. The code can be summarized by the following table. To encode or decode a message, just start with the letter in a blue row and replace it with the letter immediately beneath it. For example, "BVH" would be "YES."

A	B	C	D	E	F	G	H	I	J	K	L	M
Z	Y	X	W	V	U	T	S	R	Q	P	O	N
N	O	P	Q	R	S	T	U	V	W	X	Y	Z
M	L	K	J	I	H	G	F	E	D	C	B	A

DECODE THIS:

GSV ORLM, GSV DRGXS, ZMW GSV DZIWILYV

ANSWER

A CAVE CREATION

Recruits train in the Computer Animated Virtual Experience, also known as the CAVE. Inside, you can be immersed in any environment, from the Arctic tundra to a rainforest to a remote tropical island. Design an adventure for your team in the CAVE. Where you go is only limited by your imagination!

NUMBER
CRUNCHING

Fill in all of the empty squares so that the numbers 1 through 6 appear only once in each row, column, and box.

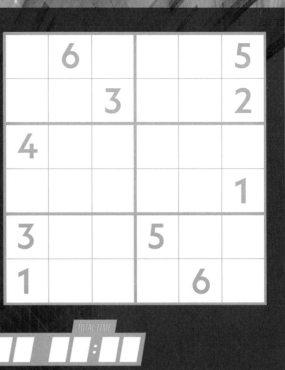

WORD *PLAY*

Every square, row, and column in this puzzle must contain one of each letter in the word BRAINY. If you complete the puzzle correctly, the letters in the diagonal squares will spell out a word that means "a computer coding system using the digits 0 and 1."

TIME IT! TIME YOURSELF TO SEE HOW FAST YOU CAN COMPLETE BOTH PUZZLES. DID YOU BEAT YOUR TIME FROM ROUND 1?

CODE *WRITER*

Solving ciphers is fun—but so is writing coded messages to your friends! Copy this symbol cipher and give it to your friend. Then you can write messages back and forth to each other and nobody will know how to decipher them unless they have the key (or are also a master codebreaker, of course).

A B C   J K L   S   W

D E F   M N O   T U   X Y

G H I   P Q R   V   Z

PRACTICE WRITING YOUR FIRST CODED MESSAGE HERE:

// TIP FROM EMMETT //

When you write something in code, you are practicing the science of encryption. This word comes from the Greek word "kryptos," which means "hidden."

DRAW SAILOR

S ailor York was one of the first recruits Cruz met when he arrived at the Academy. Now she goes on missions with him as part of Team Cousteau. Follow the steps to learn how to draw Sailor. You'll need a sharp pencil (so keep a sharpener nearby) and a good eraser. Remember to start by sketching lightly so you can erase your guidelines and fine-tune your final drawing in the space on the right.

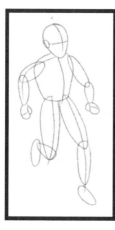

STEP ONE

Drawing an image in profile (from the side, like this image of Sailor) is a great way to practice drawing facial features. Draw guidelines to help you place elements in your drawing. Sketch an oval for the head and overlapping shapes for the body, arms, and legs as shown.

STEP TWO

Create basic shapes for the body. Make sure you sketch lightly because you will be erasing your guidelines when you fine-tune your work.

STEP THREE

Add details to the face, and remember that the eyes are actually halfway down the head! Add details to the hair, clothing, and hands.

STEP FOUR

Finalize your drawing by shading to add dimension. Erase your guidelines and add color if you like!

DRAW SAILOR HERE

ROCK
CLIMBING ➤

To complete Dr. Legrand's outdoor obstacle course, you'll need to scale up the side of a rock wall—if you don't wipe out before you get to the top! Look closely at these two rock walls. There are 15 differences between the two images. Circle the ones you find.

MINERALS OF THE
GRAND CANYON

The recruits are now on a training expedition in the Grand Canyon to study geology with Dr. Modi, professor of geography and astronomy at the Academy. There, they will find layers of rocks and minerals that are millions—and even billions—of years old. Find the names of the minerals hidden in this puzzle. Look up, down, backward, and diagonally, and circle the words you find.

```
A I L X Y C S S I Z T R A U Q
R S E L I X I L N P I T M A E
P I C T L L C E L A H S U L N
P I E T I N A R G P A L S O I
P N A C E R L I E A T E P N V
E I A F A T Y L P T T T Y I I
N G T R I R L P P I S N G R L
L O A C E F A A N T I I M J O
J M C L H Z L O S E N L R A A
X T T R L B M U E K Z F A D A
M B T I I I L X O L C C I E C
V A H B L Z N E A R L O T I I
E T I M O L O D N R I A R T M
N E T I C L A C V D O T U E M
S A N D S T O N E E E B E N D
```

APATITE
BORAX
CALCITE
DOLOMITE
FLINT
FLUORITE
GRANITE
GYPSUM
JADEITE
LIMONITE
MICA
OLIVINE
PITCHBLENDE
PYRITE
QUARTZ
ROCK SALT
SANDSTONE
SHALE
SILICA
ZIRCON

THE SECRET *BOX* !?

Cruz's aunt Marisol gave him a box of things gathered up from his mom's office. Inside it, he found some mysterious items along with some common office supplies. Connect the dots to reveal one of the objects Cruz's mom left behind for him. Could it be a clue?

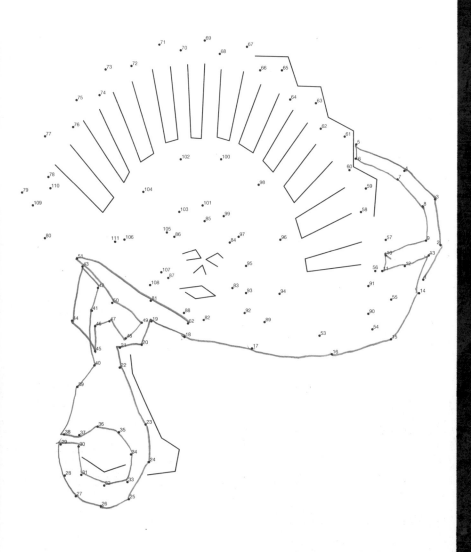

BY THE *NUMBERS*

Are you ready for your final number pyramid? To solve this puzzle, write a number in each empty square. Every square in the pyramid must contain a value exactly equal to the total of the two squares immediately beneath it.

	76

| 11 | | 12 | 9 | 6 |

DID YOU IMPROVE YOUR TIME AS YOU WORKED THROUGH ALL THE NUMBER PYRAMIDS?

START TIME ☐☐ : ☐☐   END TIME ☐☐ : ☐☐   TOTAL TIME ☐☐ : ☐☐

MISSION: *DECODABLE*

Decode this message to find out where your team of recruits is headed next.

In this code, every letter has been replaced by a different letter of the alphabet, as shown in the table below. To encode a message, start with a letter in the green row and replace it with the letter immediately beneath it. Or to decode a message, start with a letter in the white row and replace it with the letter immediately above it.

A	B	C	D	E	F	G	H	I	J	K	L	M
D	E	F	G	H	I	J	K	L	M	N	O	P
N	O	P	Q	R	S	T	U	V	W	X	Y	Z
Q	R	S	T	U	V	W	X	Y	Z	A	B	C

DECODE THE FOLLOWING MESSAGE:
PHHW DW WKH VRXWK EDVH FDPS RQ PRXQW HYHUHVW

ANSWER

ANIMALS OF THE HIMALAYA

Mount Everest is part of the Himalaya mountain chain in Asia. It is home to many animals that have adapted to live in high, cold mountain peaks. Can you unscramble the names of some of these amazing creatures?

ONWARD SLOPE	MR ATOM
SEEK DRUM	YAWL KID
DREAD PAN	USE HELP BE
REGAIN BAT	AN ALKALI BY A CHAMBER
A LOW BIRD	JUDGE PIN PRISM

WORD BANK

BLUE SHEEP	MARMOT	WILD BOAR
GIANT BEAR	MUSK DEER	WILD YAK
HIMALAYAN BLACK BEAR	RED PANDA	
JUMPING SPIDER	SNOW LEOPARD	

TRIVIA TIME

How well do you know the characters, places, and stories of Explorer Academy? Take this quiz to find out. Circle the answer to each question. Then check the answer key at the end to see how well you scored.

1 **Which Hawaiian island is Cruz from?**
a. Hawaii
b. Oahu
c. Maui
d. Kauai

2 **Who is the president of Explorer Academy?**
a. Dr. Marisol Coronado
b. Taryn Secliff
c. Dr. Regina Hightower
d. Dr. Kalpak Modi

3 What is one thing Sailor has not said?
a. "Cracker!"
b. "Crummy!"
c. "Crikey!"
d. "Sweet as!"

4 Which of these recruits is not a member of Team Cousteau?
a. Zane Patrick
b. Dugan Marsh
c. Sailor York
d. Bryndis Jónsdóttir

5 What room do Cruz and Emmett share at the Academy?
a. the Victoria Falls room
b. the Grand Canyon room
c. the Great Barrier Reef room
d. the Mount Everest room

6 What do all recruits wear on their wrist?
a. an Open Sesame band
b. a fitness tracker
c. a mini hologram projector
d. an Original Science band

7 What is the name of Cruz's honeybee drone?
a. Buzz
b. Honey
c. Mell
d. Spy

8 Which recruit gets seasick on *Orion*?
a. Cruz
b. Emmett
c. Bryndis
d. Dugan

9 Who likes to send Cruz coded messages on postcards?
a. his dad
b. his Aunt Marisol
c. his friend Lani
d. Dr. Hightower

10 What activates when you touch the planet Earth symbol on your Academy uniform?
a. a personal GPS system
b. a cloaking device
c. a communicator
d. a protective shield

11 What is the name of the company that is after Cruz?
a. Quasar
b. Narwhal
c. Renshaw
d. Nebula

12 Who is the captain of *Orion*?
a. Captain Iskandar
b. Captain Cook
c. Captain Magellan
d. Captain Ishikawa

ADD UP YOUR SCORE!

0–4: APPLICANT You have applied to the Academy, but you might not get in this year. Better luck next time!

5–9: RECRUIT You have a good general knowledge of Explorer Academy. You'll learn more the more you train.

10–12: NORTH STAR WINNER You are a good student who really knows Explorer Academy. You win the North Star trivia award!

YOUR SCORE =

ANSWER KEY: GIVE YOURSELF ONE POINT FOR EACH CORRECT ANSWER.
1. D; 2. C; 3. B; 4. A; 5. D; 6. A; 7. C; 8. B; 9. B; 10. A; 11. D; 12. A.

\\ ACTIVITY BOOK \\ 97

GALACTIC CHALLENGE

A sinister company called Nebula is out to get Cruz! A nebula is also a term for a cloud of dust and gas in space. Do you know the names of these other astronomical terms? See how many answers you can fill in.

ACROSS

1. A system of objects orbiting around a central star
4. Travel in a circle or ellipse around another object
7. A large collection of stars, held together by gravity; the Milky Way is one of these
8. A space rock that burns up in the atmosphere
10. A mass of ice and dust that orbits a star, with a "tail" traveling behind it
11. A natural satellite that orbits a planet
12. A very large body that moves in a circular or elliptical orbit around a star; Earth is one of these

DOWN

2. Gases close to a planet's surface, held there by gravity
3. A huge, burning ball of gas that lights nearby planets
5. An incredibly dense area of space formed by a collapsed planet, which is so dark that light cannot escape from it
6. A rock that orbits a star, but is smaller than a planet
9. Another name for a star; our planet orbits this

1
2
3
4
5
6
7
8
9
10
11
12

WORD BANK

Here are the entries you'll need to place in the grid—it's up to you to figure out which entry goes with which clue!

ASTEROID	MOON
ATMOSPHERE	ORBIT
BLACK HOLE	PLANET
COMET	SOLAR SYSTEM
GALAXY	STAR
METEOR	SUN

A **NEBULA** MIGHT BE MADE OF DUST, BUT SOME ARE REALLY BEAUTIFUL. ONE OF THE MOST FAMOUS IS CALLED THE **CAT'S EYE NEBULA,** NAMED FOR ITS SHAPE AND ITS BRIGHT, GLOWING COLORS.

CONGRATULATIONS!

You have made it to the final hurdle, with just one last message to decode.

This final message will test many of the code-cracking skills you have learned so far, so fingers crossed you've been paying attention!

The secret message consists of four parts. Solve each part, and then copy it into the matching area in the message box at the bottom of the opposite page. So, for example, when you have cracked the red code, copy your answer into the red box at the bottom right.

[THE RED BOX]

This code looks familiar. It's one that Cruz's mom used to write a secret message to him. Can you decode what it says?

[THE BLUE BOX]

You've seen this before, too: a code that always uses two-digit numbers. You used it to decode a message that a Nebula agent had dropped!

24 45   45 11 31 15 44   45 35

HINT: STUCK? CHECK BACK TO THE FOLLOWING PAGES: RED CODE: PAGE 6; BLUE CODE: PAGE 14, YELLOW CODE: PAGE 63, GREEN CODE: PAGE 51

This is a tricky one! What could these two numbers mean? Do you think they are using the same code that Professor Coronado slipped you in Washington, D.C.?

28 27 6

(THE GREEN BOX)

It's nearly time to finish. Wait a second ... time! Doesn't that remind you of a code you came across somewhere before?

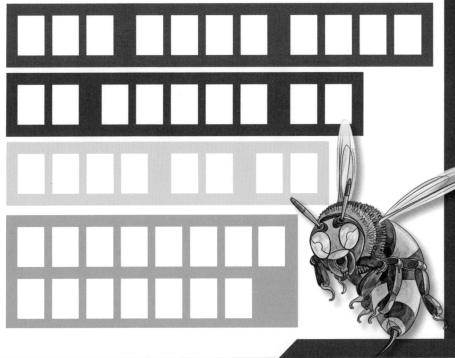

ANSWERS

PG. 6 CODEBREAKER
WELCOME TO THE ACADEMY

PG. 7 STOKED TO SURF

PG. 10 ALOHA, HAWAII!

PG. 11 PIXEL SURFBOARD

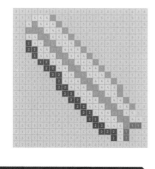

PG. 12-13 THE ADVENTURE BEGINS

PG. 14 A MYSTERIOUS MESSAGE
DO NOT LET CRUZ CORONADO OUT OF
YOUR SIGHT!

PG. 15 ON THE RUN

PG. 16 FIND THE SPY!
THE MUSEUM

PG. 20–21 EXPLORING EGYPT

PG. 25 FIND THE FISH

PG. 22–23 HIDDEN RELICS

PG. 28 NUMBER CRUNCHING

5	3	6	2	1	4
1	2	4	3	6	5
3	4	1	6	5	2
2	6	5	4	3	1
4	5	3	1	2	6
6	1	2	5	4	3

PG. 28 WORDPLAY

H	S	L	E	U	T
T	U	E	H	S	L
E	T	S	L	H	U
U	L	H	T	E	S
S	E	T	U	L	H
L	H	U	S	T	E

PG. 24 ALL ABOARD *ORION*!
STORAGE, MINI CAVE, ATRIUM, BRIDGE DECK, OBSERVATION DECK, CLASSROOMS, GALLEY, LABS, LOUNGE, CONTROL ROOM, SCUBA, BRIDGE, SICK BAY, FACULTY OFFICES

PG. 24 LAND HO!

1. BOAT
2. BOLT
3. BOLD
4. BALD
5. BAND
6. LAND

PG. 35 LAND OF ICE AND SNOW

PG. 29 WHO'S WHO?

PG. 30-31 PLOT YOUR ADVENTURE
1. MEXICO; 2. BRAZIL; 3. ICELAND;
4. CAMEROON; 5. MADAGASCAR; 6. INDIA;
7. AUSTRALIA; 8. JAPAN

PG. 34 BUNDLE UP AND GET MOVING

PG. 36 CAVE CONUNDRUM

PG. 37 THE EXPLORERS' MOTTO
TO DISCOVER. TO INNOVATE. TO PROTECT.

PG. 40 COLORFUL MOOD

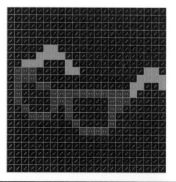

PG. 41 INCREDIBLE EXPLORERS

PG. 42–43 SURVIVAL TRAINING

HURDLE

MONKEY BARS

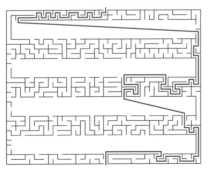

CARGO NET

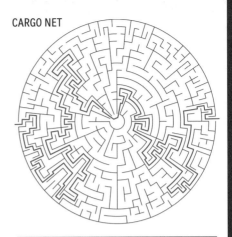

PG. 44 WHAT'S THE WORD?
1. CAT
2. COAT
3. ACTOR
4. CARROT
5. TRACTOR

PG. 45 MIGRATING MARVELS

UNSCRAMBLED NAME: MONARCH BUTTERFLIES

PG. 46 ANCIENT EXPEDITION
MEET AT THE EL CASTILLO PYRAMID
AT MIDNIGHT

[ANSWERS]

PG. 47 EXPLORE MEXICO

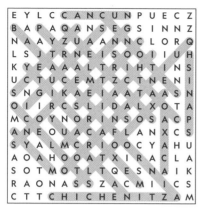

PG. 54-55 IN THE LIBRARY

PG. 50 WAVE THE FLAG
THE SAHARA IN NORTH AFRICA

PG. 51 WATCH THE CLOCK
A SCORCHING ONE HUNDRED TWENTY °F

PG. 52-53 ANIMALS OF THE SAHARA

PG. 58-59 EXPERT EXPLORERS

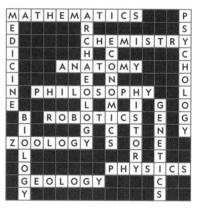

PG. 62 WHAT'S THE WORD?
1. LIE
2. ISLE
3. SLIDE
4. SAILED
5. DETAILS

PG. 63 THE CULPER CODE
MEET AT DAWN IN FRONT OF THE
CAPITOL BUILDING

PG. 64 SUBTERRANEAN EXPEDITION

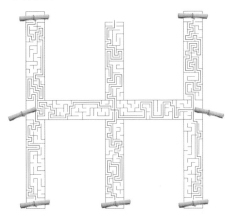

PG. 70 WHAT'S THE SECRET WORD?

PG. 65 A PUZZLE OF PRESIDENTS

PG. 66–67 THE STREETS OF D.C.
1. NATIONAL WORLD WAR II MEMORIAL
2. LINCOLN MEMORIAL
3. MARTIN LUTHER KING, JR.
4. NATIONAL MUSEUM OF
   AMERICAN HISTORY

PG. 71 BY THE NUMBERS

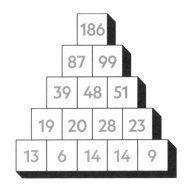

PG. 74 ANIMALS OF NEW ZEALAND
UNSCRAMBLED NAMES: LONG-TAILED BAT,
ARCHEY'S FROG

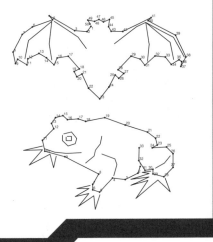

[ANSWERS]

PG. 75 EXPLORE NEW ZEALAND

PG. 76 FIORDLAND NATIONAL PARK

PG. 77 BY THE NUMBERS

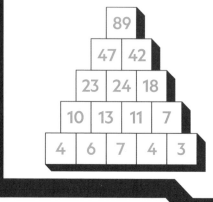

PG. 80 DESTINATION: DUGAN'S HOMETOWN
SANTA FE, NEW MEXICO

PG. 81 UP, UP, AND AWAY

PG. 82 ANIMALS OF NEW MEXICO
1. JAVELINA; 2. BOBCAT; 3. PORCUPINE;
4. COUGAR; 5. ROADRUNNER; 6. JACKRABBIT;
7. GILA MONSTER; 8. BIGHORN SHEEP

PG. 83 TINY TECH

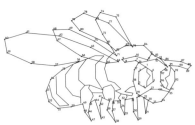

PG. 83 THE CLUE IN THE BOOK
THE LION, THE WITCH, AND THE WARDROBE

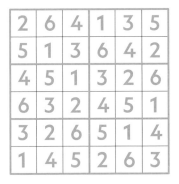

2	6	4	1	3	5
5	1	3	6	4	2
4	5	1	3	2	6
6	3	2	4	5	1
3	2	6	5	1	4
1	4	5	2	6	3

B	Y	R	N	A	I
N	I	A	Y	B	R
I	A	N	R	Y	B
R	B	Y	A	I	N
Y	N	I	B	R	A
A	R	B	I	N	Y

```
A I L X Y C S S I Z T R A U Q
R S E L I X I L N P I T M A E
P I C T L L C E L A H S U L N
P I E T I N A R G P A L S O I
P N A C E R L I E A T E P N V
E I A F A T Y L P T T T Y I I
N G T R I R L P P I S N G R L
L O A C E F A A N T I I M J O
J M C L H Z L O S E N L R A A
X T T R L B M U E K Z F A D A
M B T I I I L X O L C C I E C
V A H B L Z N E A R L O T I I
E T I M O L O D N R I A R T M
N E T I C L A C V D O T U E M
S A N D S T O N E E E B E N D
```

PG. 94 BY THE NUMBERS

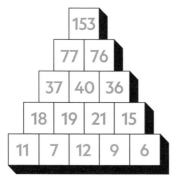

	153			
	77	76		
	37	40	36	
	18	19	21	15
11	7	12	9	6

PG. 95 MISSION: DECODABLE
MEET AT THE SOUTH BASE CAMP ON MOUNT EVEREST

PG. 95 ANIMALS OF THE HIMALAYA
SNOW LEOPARD, MUSK DEER, RED PANDA, GIANT BEAR, WILD BOAR, MARMOT, WILD YAK, BLUE SHEEP, HIMALAYAN BLACK BEAR, JUMPING SPIDER

PG. 98-99 GALACTIC CHALLENGE

PG. 100-101 FINAL PUZZLE
THE RED BOX USES THE SPIRAL CODE FROM PAGE 6, AND THE ANSWER IS "YOU HAVE WHAT."
THE BLUE BOX USES THE POLYBIUS SQUARE FROM PAGE 14, AND THE ANSWER IS "IT TAKES TO."
THE YELLOW BOX USES THE CULPER CODE FROM PAGE 63, AND THE ANSWER IS "MAKE IT AT."
THE GREEN BOX USES THE SEMAPHORE CLOCK CODE FROM PAGE 51, AND THE ANSWER IS "EXPLORER ACADEMY."

WHEN YOU WRITE ALL THE DECODED MESSAGES TOGETHER, YOU REVEAL THE FINAL SOLUTION: **YOU HAVE WHAT IT TAKES TO MAKE IT AT EXPLORER ACADEMY**

[PHOTO CREDITS]

All illustrations by Scott Plumb unless otherwise noted below.

DS=Dreamstime; SS=Shutterstock;
Cover (hedge maze), Gualberto Becerra/SS; (pencils in cup), Natali Zakharova/SS; various (pixel art), campincool/SS; various (topo map lines), DamienGeso/SS; 1 (pixel art), polovinkin/SS; 1, Pius Lee/SS; 2 (LO), Elitravo/DS; 2 (UP), Matthew Rakola; 5, Gualberto Becerra/SS; 6 (LO), Jule_Berlin/SS; 6 (pixel art), Dmitrii Vlasov/SS; 7 (BACKGROUND), EpicStockMedia/SS; 7 (UP), Steve Collender/SS; 8 (pixel art summer theme), derter/SS; 10-11, Ellensmile/DS; 10 (UP), Videowokart/SS; 10 (LO), Brand X; 11 (LO), James Steidl/SS; 12 (pixel art surfer), derGriza/SS; 13 (pixel art Iceland theme), derGriza/SS; 14 (pixel art science theme), derGriza/SS; 14 (BACKGROUND), Alfonso de Tomas/SS; 15, Pavel Mitrofanov/SS; 16 (old world map for binoculars), RTimages/SS; 16 (binoculars), Rob Hyrons/SS; 18-19 (pixel art gears), Artistdesign29/SS; 20-21 (pixel art Egyptian theme), polovinkin/SS; 20-21, Pius Lee/SS; 22-23, Iconotec/Alamy Stock Photo; 24-25, Irina Markova/SS; 25 (pixel art transportation theme), VectorPixelStar/SS; 25 (LO), Tanya Puntti/SS; 27, VectorPixelStar/SS; 30 (old world map for binoculars), RTimages/SS; 30 (binoculars), Rob Hyrons/SS; 32, David Ashley/SS; 33 (UP), Sergey Novikov/SS; 33 (LO), Normana Karia/SS; 34-36, Jamen Percy/SS; 39 (CTR RT), Halyna Parinova/SS; 39 (CTR LE), Militarist/SS; 39 (UP), Dario Lo Presti/SS; 39 (LO), Eileen Tweedy/REX/SS; 40-41, pixelparticle/SS; 40 (pixel art summer vacation theme), kmarfu/SS; 46-47, Victor Torres/SS; 46 (UP), Irafael/SS; 46 (LO), Elitravo/DS; 47 (UP), railway fx/SS; 47 (LO), Jose Ignacio Soto/SS; 50, Sandra Van Der Steen/DS; 50-51, Pavel Nesvadba/SS; 51, RTimages/SS; 52-53, Wrangel/DS; 52 (UP), Protasov AN/SS; 52 (LO), Anolis01/iStockphoto/Getty Images; 53, Jarpz/SS; 56-57, Sundari/SS; 57, gan chaonan/SS; 58-59 (BACKGROUND), Zoezoe33/SS; 58 (RT), Anton Mykhailovsk/SS; 58, Nitr/SS; 59, Darya Hrybouskaya/SS; 60 (3a), svic/SS; 60 (3b), AP Photo; 60 (3d), Corbis via Getty Images; 61, Top Vector Studio/SS; 61 (CTR RT), Georgios Kollidas/SS; 61, AP Photo; 61 (LO), Library of Congress Prints and Photographs Division; 61 (UP), Library of Congress Prints and Photographs Division; 62-63, Pozdeyev Vitaly/SS; 64-65, Joseph Sohm/SS; 64, Ulkastudio/SS; 65, Everett Historical/SS; 66 (old world map for binoculars), RTimages/SS; 66 (binoculars), Rob Hyrons/SS; 70-71, Chim/SS; 70 (fingerprints), David Alary/SS; 72, Eduardo Rivero/SS; 73, Chansom Pantip/SS; 74-75, Olga Danylenko/SS; 75 (UP), reptiles4all/SS; 75 (LO), GlobalP/iStockphoto/Getty Images; 76-77, Christopher Meder/SS; 79 (Polaroid photo frame), Ninell/SS; 82 (LO RT), Matauw/DS; 82 (UP), Chris Lorenz/DS; 82-83, kojihirano/SS; 82 (LO LE), Tom Reichner/SS; 90, Rachael Hamm; 92 (LO LE), Kongsky/DS; 92-93 (BACKGROUND), Keneva Photograph/SS; 92 (LO RT), Juraj Kovac/SS; 92 (UP), carlos-delacalle/SS; 98 (pixel art space theme), anna_wizard/SS; 98-99 (BACKGROUND), Anatolii Vasilev/SS; 98 (LO), David Aguilar; 99 (cipher), Eileen Tweedy/REX/SS; 100 (cipher), Eileen Tweedy/REX/SS

Since 1888, the National Geographic Society has funded more than 12,000 research, exploration, and preservation projects around the world. The Society receives funds from National Geographic Partners, LLC, funded in part by your purchase. A portion of the proceeds from this book supports this vital work. To learn more, visit natgeo.com/info.

NATIONAL GEOGRAPHIC and Yellow Border Design are trademarks of the National Geographic Society, used under license.

For more information, visit nationalgeographic.com, call 1-800-647-5463, or write to the following address:

National Geographic Partners
1145 17th Street N.W.
Washington, D.C. 20036-4688 U.S.A.

Visit us online at nationalgeographic.com/books

For librarians and teachers: ngchildrensbooks.org

More for kids from National Geographic: natgeokids.com

National Geographic Kids magazine inspires children to explore their world with fun yet educational articles on animals, science, nature, and more. Using fresh storytelling and amazing photography, *Nat Geo Kids* shows kids ages 6 to 14 the fascinating truth about the world—and why they should care. **kids.nationalgeographic.com/subscribe**

For information about special discounts for bulk purchases, please contact National Geographic Books Special Sales: specialsales@natgeo.com

For rights or permissions inquiries, please contact National Geographic Books Subsidiary Rights: bookrights@natgeo.com

Designed by Rachael Hamm Plett, Moduza Design

Trade paperback ISBN: 978-1-4263-3461-0

The publisher would like to thank Tracey West, writer; Dr. Gareth Moore, puzzle creator; Jen Agresta, project editor; Becky Baines, editorial director; Kate Hale, executive editor; Michaela Weglinski, assistant editor; Eva Absher-Schantz, art director; Lori Epstein, photo director; Joan Gossett, editorial production manager; Alix Inchausti, production editor; and Anne LeongSon and Gus Tello, design production assistants.

Printed in Hong Kong
19/PPHK/1

GET IN ON THE ADVENTURE!

Were you there for Cruz's first day at Explorer Academy? Start at the beginning. Meet Cruz, Lani, Emmett, and Sailor, and discover why Explorer Academy is the coolest school on the planet in *The Nebula Secret* and *The Falcon's Feather* ... and beyond! Get the story behind Cruz's mysterious mission, practice your new codebreaking skills, and explore the world!